The Owl in the Old Oak Tree and Little Squirrel Gray

by A S Tarantiuk

Grosvenor House
Publishing Limited

This book is published by
Grosvenor House Publishing Ltd
Link House
140 The Broadway, Tolworth, Surrey, KT6 7HT.
www.grosvenorhousepublishing.co.uk

A CIP record for this book
is available from the British Library

ISBN 978-1-83975-933-8

THE OWL IN THE OLD OAK TREE AND LITTLE SQUIRREL GRAY

Across the sea of yellow that is the buttercup meadow. Through the forest and across the brook you begin to see the old oak wood. Deep within the bluebell filled wood there an oak tree stood. What a magical place it seemed to be underneath this old oak tree.

Little Gray lived the other side of the oak wood, with his
mum and sisters in a small neighbourhood.

His favourite time was before school begun
when he could run around with his sisters and
have lots of fun.

But little Gray felt misunderstood. When it came to school he was just no good.

He would practice so hard for the spelling tests he took, and he really wanted to be able to read a book. Even his teachers thought he was hopeless, telling his mum he just didn't seem to focus.

One day he'd just had enough, he couldn't cope with anymore school stuff. He just wanted to get away, and not think about school even if it was just for the day.

So off he went on his way with the words of his classmates going round in his head on replay.

"Gray can't read" they shouted.

"He can't even spell his name" the older squirrels spouted.

By the time little grey had reached the base of an old oak tree
he had started to chant aloud a simple plea.

"Oh I wish I was clever too...
oh I wish, I wish, I was clever too."

Twit woo

Suddenly a voice took Gray quite by surprise.
As the sun was shining so bright in his eyes.
"twit twoo twit twoo, my dear squirrel why
are you so blue."

9

Before asking Gray the same question as before, an owl appeared at a little front door.

"Well" said little Gray, "I cannot read from a book or spell my name, it gets so bad the words start to look the same"

Little Gray's eyes started to fill with tears, as he slumped to the floor overwhelmed by his fears.

"To be normal like others would be my dream". And with those words Gray's tears started to stream.

The owl comforted little Gray as he cried
and after he had calmed down a little,
he invited him inside.

Little Gray took a seat in the living room of the old oak tree, while the owl made them a pot of tea.

"So", said the owl "do tell me more, why do you think your reading is so poor?"

14

"Well", said little Gray, "Its hard to explain but the words jump around on the page you see, and I mix up my B's and D's".

"Ah," said the owl "I see what you say but you really must stop thinking this way. It's quite normal for us to all learn differently, but that's not a reflection upon your ability."

Little Gray had a sip of this drink, as he took in the owls words, and started to think.

The Owl and Gray sat and talked for a while, and slowly little Gray began to smile.

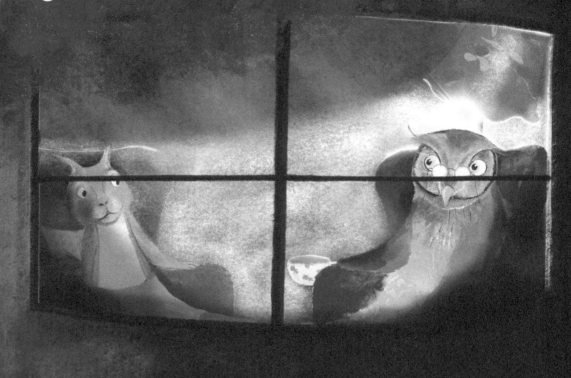

As the time went on they talked about everything, and as they did the Owl started to notice a few things.

With a smile on his face the owl announced, "well reading might be difficult for you but you have many other gifts too."

"Have you noticed; you can piece a problem together like a puzzle in your head. When others face this, this is something they dread."

"No" replied Little Squirrel Gray "I thought everyone tackled problems this way".

"I'm in awe of how you can create whole worlds in your mind's eye, others can't do this no matter how hard they try".

"Really" replied Gray, "I thought everyone could see things this way"

"It really is amazing how you see connections between lots of things, they just seem to appear in your mind like brightly coloured string."

"Is it?" Replied Gray, "I thought everyone's mind worked this way."

"You are as clever as the others you see, you just need to do things a little differently."

"When you try to read change the colour
of the page.

When you need to remember a name, think of something
connected to help jog your brain."

"And when you want to remember a spelling, draw pictures of the word in your mind.

Using little tricks like this will stop you feeling like you're falling behind."

"If there is one bit of wisdom I can share with you. Is that you may work differently but you can do great things too".

Little Squirrel Gray's face filled with joy,

as he realised, he was the same as any other schoolboy.

"I'm so glad I came here today and learned that I am not stupid as the other squirrels say. Thank you, Mr Owl, for talking to me today, but I really should be on my way".

When little Gray arrived home, his mum
hugged him tight, and as she did, he
apologised for giving her a fright.

28

While little Squirrel Gray got ready for bed, he continued to tell his mum all that Owl had said.

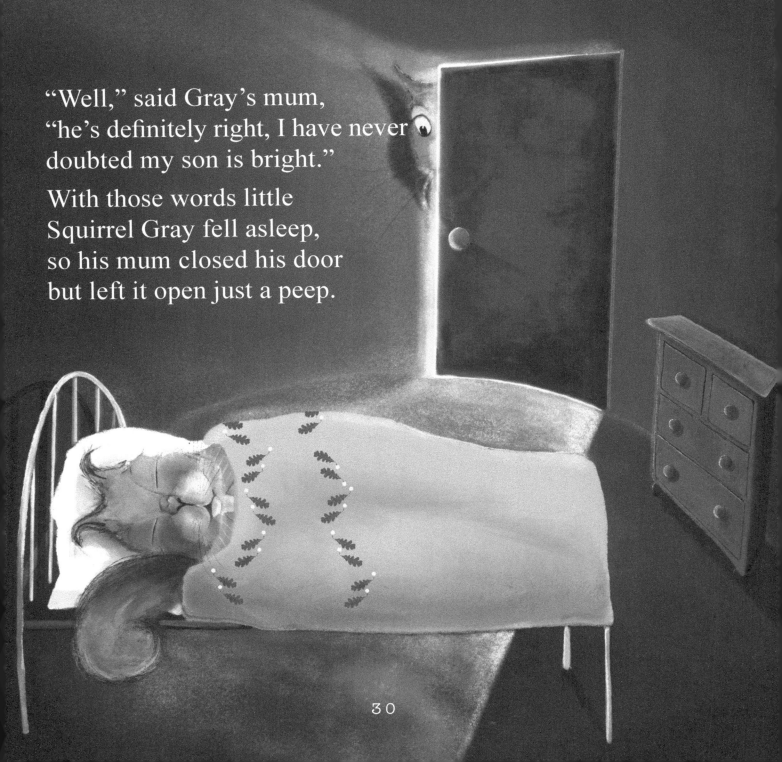

"Well," said Gray's mum,
"he's definitely right, I have never
doubted my son is bright."

With those words little
Squirrel Gray fell asleep,
so his mum closed his door
but left it open just a peep.

Not sure how it came to be, but little Gray was very glad that the wise owl lived in that old oak tree.

The end

Lightning Source UK Ltd.
Milton Keynes UK
UKHW050628260422
402057UK00008B/112